Walrus's *Adventure*
in Alphabet Town

by Janet Riehecky
illustrated by Diana Magnuson

created by Wing Park Publishers

CHILDRENS PRESS ®
CHICAGO

Library of Congress Cataloging-in-Publication Data

Riehecky, Janet.
    Walrus's adventure in Alphabet Town / by Janet Riehecky ;
illustrated by Diana Magnuson.
       p.   cm. — (Read around Alphabet Town)
    Summary: One Wednesday when Walrus is bored, he decides
to have a water party and invites his friends Whale, Woodchuck
and Woodpecker.
   ISBN 0-516-05423-6
   [1. Alphabet.   2. Walruses—Fiction.   3. Parties—Fiction.] I.
Magnuson, Diana, ill.   II. Title.   III. Series.
PZ7.R4277Wal   1992
[E]—dc 20   92-1330
                                         CIP
                                         AC

Walrus's *Adventure*

in Alphabet Town

You are now entering Alphabet Town,
With houses from "A" to "Z."
I'm going on a "W" adventure today,
So come along with me.

This is the "W" house of Alphabet
Town. Walrus lives here.

Walrus likes things that begin with
"w." He has lots of them in his house.

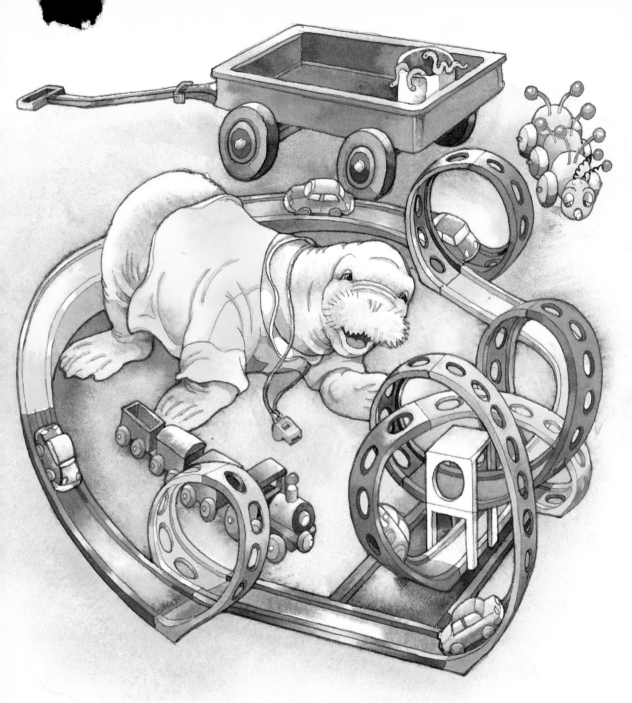

"I like wagons, whistles, worms, and wheels," says Walrus.

And most of the time, Walrus likes
Wednesdays too. But one Wednesday
he was bored.

He watched his mother do the wash.
"What can I do for fun?" asked Walrus.
"Well, we have not had a party in a
long while," said his mother.

"Would you like to plan a party?"
"Wow, would I!" said Walrus. "I will
plan a water party."

First Walrus went to see

Whale.

"Will you come to my water party?"
he asked.

"When is it?" asked Whale.
"In one week," said Walrus.
"I will come," said Whale.

Next, Walrus went to see

Woodchuck and Woodpecker.

"Will you come to my water party?"
he asked.
"We will," they said.

In one week, Walrus was ready for the
party. The weather was perfect. It was
nice and warm.

Walrus waited by the water for his friends. When they came, he said, "Welcome to my party. Let's play water tag."

Walrus almost tagged Woodchuck.
But Woodchuck wiggled away.

17

Woodpecker did not want to get her
wings wet. "I will just watch," she
said.

Then they had a contest to see who could make the biggest waves. Whale won.

"What should we do next?" asked
Woodchuck. Walrus picked up a stick.
"Let's play magic wand," he said.

"I will wave my wand and make a wish.
I wish we had a boat. Then we could
water ski."

"I will be the boat," said Whale.
Whale made a fine boat.

Soon they were hungry. Woodpecker
picked up the stick. "Now I will
make a wish," she said. "I wish we
had food."

Just then, Walrus's mother came walking down the path. She had a wagon full of

wild cherry pies.

"Wow!" said Woodpecker. "It worked!" Walrus laughed.

"I was watching from the window,"
said Walrus's mother. "You look like
you are having a wonderful time."

"We are," said Walrus. "We even found a magic wand."

Soon it was time to go home. Walrus
waved good-bye to his friends. All
the way home, he sang:

" 'W' is for water, wonderful and wet.
'W' is for Wednesday, the best one yet.
'W' is for wand and wishes that come true.
'W' is for Walrus and what he found to do."

MORE FUN WITH WALRUS

What's in a Name?

In my "w" adventure, you read many "w" words. My name begins with a "W." Many of my friends' names begin with "W" too. Here are a few.

Whitney

Wes

Wade

Winnie

Wilma

Ward

Walt

Wendy

Do you know other names that start with "W"?

Does your name start with "W"?

Walrus's Word Hunt

I like to hunt for "w" words. Can you help me find the words on this page that begin with "w"? How many are there? Can you read them?

witch

clown

cow

rainbow

kitten

gown

windmill

wolf

Can you find any words with "w" in the middle?
Can you find any with "w" at the end?
Can you find a word with no "w"?

Walrus's Favorite Things

"W" is my favorite letter. I love "w" things. Can you guess why? You can find some of my favorite "w" things in my house on page 7. How many "w" things can you find there? Can you think of more "w" things?

Now you make up a "w" adventure.